KU-154-628

"I was born in London in 1946 and grew up in a sweet shop in Essex. For several years I worked as a graphic designer, but in 1980 I decided to concentrate on writing and illustrating books for children.

My wife, Annette, and I have two grown-up children, Ben and Amanda, and we have put down roots in Suffolk.

I haven't recently counted how many books there are with my name on the cover but Percy the Park Keeper accounts for a good many of them. I'm reliably informed that they have sold more than three million copies. Hooray!

I didn't realise this when I invented Percy, but I can now see that he's very like my mum's dad, my grandpa. I even have a picture of him giving a ride to my brother and me in his old home-made wooden wheelbarrow!"

NICK BUTTERWORTH

ON THE COVER

Percy says: "One of the ducks got tangled up in some weeds. I managed to fish him out but as I was coming out of the pond I slipped and splashed into the water myself. Later when the fox saw me with my net, he asked if I had caught anything. I said, 'Yes, a duck and a cold!'"

PERCY'S FRIENDS
THE DUCKS

NICK BUTTERWORTH

TED SMART

Thanks Graham Daldry. You're a wizard.

Thanks Atholl McDonald. You're a hero!

This edition produced for The Book People Ltd, Hall Wood Avenue, Haydock, St Helens WAll 9UL

1 3 5 7 9 10 8 6 4 2

ISBN: 0 00 770016 4

Text and illustrations copyright © Nick Butterworth 2002
The author asserts the moral right to be identified as the author of the work.

A CIP catalogue record for this title is available from the British Library.
All rights reserved. No part of this publication may be reproduced, stored in a retrieval
system or transmitted in any form or by any means, electronic, mechanical, photocopying,
recording or otherwise, without the prior permission of HarperCollins Publishers Ltd,
77-85 Fulham Palace Road, Hammersmith, London W6 8JB.

The HarperCollins website address is: www.harpercollins.co.uk

Printed and bound in China

MY FRIENDS THE DUCKS

These two ducks used to live on a farm near the park but one day, they landed 'splash' in front of me and they have stayed here ever since.

They are completely devoted to each other. They fuss and quack over everything. If you hear them you might think that they are having a heated argument but if you listen more closely, you'll see that it's more like a heated agreement!

They live on the lake close to the big tree house. But they do spend more time outside the park than the other animals. They visit friends and sometimes their friends visit them. This can lead to confusion...

When the ducks' friends come to visit they usually come in ones or twos. Once or twice, three or four have turned up.

Just imagine my surprise one day, when nineteen, yes, nineteen of them suddenly appeared in the playground! Altogether, that made . . . er, well, what's nineteen add two . . ? It's certainly a lot of ducks!

They were having a wonderful
time. The noise of their quacking
and squawking was amazing. They all
looked so much alike. It was almost
impossible to tell who was who. But, if you
look carefully, I think you might be able to
pick out the two who live in the park.

THE DUCKS REALLY LIKE . . .

Baskets! I can't think why. Perhaps it's
because they remind them of nests.
The fox likes baskets too. Picnic baskets.

Rain. Sometimes, when it rains,
people say, "Nice weather for ducks."
The ducks would agree.

THE DUCKS DON'T LIKE . . .

Autumn time. It's then that many of their
friends fly away to find somewhere warmer
for the winter. Some never come back.

Boats. They would much rather be swimming
in the water than afloat in a boat!

The ducks are wonderful ice skaters.
Just go down to the lake on a
winter's afternoon and watch.
You won't be disappointed.
And you won't be alone.
When the ducks take to the
ice, people stop and stare.
And they gasp...

Spinning and twirling, the ducks dance
beautifully together, slowly at first, now
more quickly, flowing easily over the ice...
now in a graceful life, she seems to weigh
almost nothing...such perfect timing, so
artistic. It's hard to believe that these are the
same two who, only ten minutes ago, asked
if I had any stale breadcrumbs. Full marks.

I've got lots of pictures in my photo album.

The perfect view point to take in a beautiful view.

Well, what <u>do</u> you say to a plastic duck?

Here are some I took of my good friends, the ducks.

I was glad
to see these
two friends
again after
an accident
involving
prickles.

A flypast
of ducks
for a
birthday
mouse.

Ducks like acorns. I was
surprised when I found out.
But not as surprised as the
poor squirrel who had
worked very hard to make a
large store by the edge of the
lake. Not a good place. The ducks
found the acorns and gobbled
up the lot!

Have you ever heard someone say,
"Keep your beak out of my
acorns?" Well, this is where
that saying comes from.

DUCKING

If you ever wondered why
We like to swim as much as fly,
Come to the lake! We think you'll see
Why this is where we like to be.

When we're tired of swimming round,
We turn the whole world upside down.
We stick our bottoms in the air
And find another world . . . down there.

There the watery sunlight weaves
Strange patterns through the lily leaves.
We talk to fish – we like the tale
Of how a trout once met a whale!

We play with tadpoles in the reeds
And chase each other through the weeds.
And so you see we're never stuck
For fun and games,
We simply
Duck!

FAVOURITE PLACES

Did I tell you about the ruined house in the grounds of the park? Well, there are two fountains nearby. One doesn't work at all. The other one works, but it leaks rather badly. I don't turn it on very often, but I do get it going sometimes on a hot summer's day. It's the perfect place to cool down.

Most of my animal friends like to splash about in the pool or take a shower under the fountain, although I don't think I've ever seen the badger with them.

The ducks are always first in. They love it. It really is one of their favourite places.

Of course, for the ducks, home is another favourite place. They live down by the lake next to the big tree house...

Here they are, my friends the ducks, right at the top of the tree house. It's not quite so unusual as some people think to see a duck up a tree. I would have to agree though, it's much more unusual to see one on a helter-skelter!

Read all the stories about Percy and his animal friends...

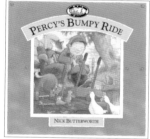

Percy toys and videos
are also available.